SO-BII-137

Contents

Little Faith

The Child of the Toy Stall

Mrs. O. F. Walton

Cover Illustration

James Converse

Cover Design

Mike Cole

Book Design

Trinda Cole

Published by:
AB Publishing, Inc.
Ithaca, MI 48847
www.abpub.com

1

The Toy Stall

$\mathcal{I}$t was market day, and everyone in that busy
town was even busier than usual. The marketplace
was crowded with people of all ages and occupa-
tions, hurrying along as if every moment was of
consequence to them, and pushing and jostling
against everyone else, as if it were quite impossible
that anyone's business could be of as much impor-
tance as theirs. It was a curious old marketplace;
not a large open square, with plenty of room to
move about between the various stalls, as in most
of our more modern towns, but a long, narrow,
old-fashioned street, with a row of stalls on each

side of the road, close to the pavement, and only just room enough between the rows for the carts and carriages to pass through.

All sorts of things might be bought at these little stalls. There was the cap stall, with innumerable caps of all sizes and shapes—caps for old men, caps for young men, caps for big boys, caps for little boys, and caps for baby boys.

There was the stocking stall, where were displayed, in tempting rows, blue stockings, white stockings, grey stockings, brown stockings, black stockings, and striped stockings. There was the bootlace stall, with its hundreds of bootlaces, hanging side by side on strings which were stretched from one side of the stall to the other. There was the basket stall, at which you could buy a clothes basket, a market basket, a fish basket, a cap basket, a fruit basket, or a dinner basket. There was the sweets stall, which was always surrounded by children who seemed to be trying to devour its contents by means of their greedy glances.

There was the gingerbread stall, which was hardly less popular, with its rows of gingerbread cats with pink eyes, and gingerbread dogs with blue eyes, and gingerbread men with no eyes at all.

There was the picture stall, which was a favorite resort for young men and women who were setting up housekeeping, containing a number of pictures of ladies and gentlemen dressed in every color of the rainbow, and surrounded by most brilliant and startling frames. And then there were numberless toy stalls, standing side by side, and all of them very much alike.

At one of these stood a man and a child, watching the faces of the people as they passed by and holding up one thing after another from the stall to tempt them to buy. The man was tall and thin, and one of his coat sleeves hung empty at his side, for he had lost his right arm.

The child had an anxious, thoughtful face and looked older than her years. She was not more than ten years old, though she might have been taken for twelve or thirteen.

Crowds of people passed the stall, but no one stopped to buy. A few turned over the things, asked their price, and then walked on again and did the same at the next stall. The man seemed very anxious to secure a purchaser and very clever in trying to suit the tastes of the various passersby: the old men and women were invited to stop to

Faith and her father at the toy stall.

examine the quality and cheapness of a pipe or a spectacle case; the mothers of families were pressed to take "just a pretty penny toy or two to the bairns at home"; the young girls were invited to buy the long strings of yellow and blue beads which were hanging across the top of the stall, and which could be made into necklaces, or bracelets, or chains, according to taste; the young men were shown cheap knives, cheap pocket combs, cheap breast pins, and cheap shirt-studs; whilst the children were called, again and again, to look at the trumpets, the dolls, the tops, the balls, and the boxes of toys with which the stall abounded.

But none of them fell into the traps so carefully laid for them. No one seemed to want anything that Friday morning. The little girl tinkled the penny bells to show how well they sounded and made Jack jump out of his box again and again, but all in vain! A child came and bought a halfpenny slate pencil, but not another halfpenny did they take the whole morning.

"Bad luck today, Faith," said the man, as they sat down on a box behind the stall to eat their scanty dinner.

"Oh, maybe it will be a bit better this afternoon," said the child. "The country folk don't care about carrying a lot of things about with them all day—we mostly take more of afternoons than mornings."

"We never take a deal at any time," said the man, gloomily, as he got up to show off his wares again.

The afternoon was cold and wet. The rain came down in torrents, and Faith shivered as she wrapped her thin faded shawl, which was becoming more drenched every moment, around her.

"Here, Faith, child," said the man, putting a piece of sacking around her, "keep thyself warm, bairn; I can hold on as long as thou art well."

It seemed of very little use their stopping in the marketplace. The people who passed along were hurrying on to get shelter from the rain and scarcely glanced at the stall as they went by. The country people had all gone home, and the marketplace was becoming very empty. The owners of the cap stall, of the basket stall, and of the bootlace stall were hastily packing up their wares and preparing to depart.

But still the man and the child held on. The toys were not getting wet—that was one good thing. The covering of the stall was waterproof, and there was no wind. So hour after hour they waited, hoping to the last that customers might come to the stall.

It was quite dark now, and the few stall keepers who remained had lighted their naphtha lights and hung them up under cover of their stalls. The passersby became very few and far between as the night went on. At last the great church clock over their heads struck eleven, and the market keeper came to see the lights put out and the street cleared.

The man and the child packed up the unsold articles in their various cases, without saying a single word to each other, and put out their lights. Then the man put the boxes on a handcart and took them to a house near, where a friend of his lived who took charge of them till the next market day.

The child was white and tired and seemed as downcast as the man. He gave her his hand when all was stowed away, and then they walked on towards their home.

The streets were very quiet now, for it was half-past eleven, and they met very few people on their way. They had gone down several streets before either of them spoke. The man was the first to break the silence.

"Only sixpence the whole day, Faith," he said. "We never had such bad luck as that before!"

"What will Mrs. Gubbins say?" said the child.

"Aye!" he said. "What will Mrs. Gubbins say? Well, well, we can't help it; we've done our best, anyhow."

But he was evidently as much afraid of Mrs. Gubbins' displeasure as she was.

At last they stopped at a door in a dirty, miserable street. The door was unbolted, so the man went in, and Faith followed him up a long, rickety staircase, which seemed as if it would give way beneath their weight.

They passed two landings, and then they reached a door at the top of the high house. The man paused for a moment, as if he were almost afraid to enter.

"Can't be helped," he said, almost with a groan, as he went in. The child followed him with a timid, shrinking step.

It was a dirty, forlorn room. The floor was rough and uneven and full of holes, and the rotten boards creaked and strained as they walked across them. The walls were damp and discolored and covered with filth; the little window had not a whole pane to boast of but was patched up with rags and newspaper.

There was hardly any furniture in the room, only a small round table, two or three broken boxes, and one dilapidated armchair. In this chair, with her feet on the fender and her hands stretched out over the fire, sat an old woman. Her back was turned to the door, and she never looked round as the man and the child came in.

Faith crept quietly past her to a corner of the room where three children were lying asleep under a dirty blanket. They had lain down to sleep with their clothes on, unwashed, uncombed, and uncared for. They had no mother.

"Oh, if she could see them!" said Faith to herself, as she stooped down to kiss a little grimy, sticky hand which was peeping out from a corner of the dirty blanket. "Oh, if she could only see them, whatever would she say! It's to be hoped folks in heaven doesn't know what goes on."

The man sat down on a box by the table and leaned his head on his hand. There was a strong smell of gin in the room; the old woman had been having her supper just before they came in.

"Well," she said, without turning round, "the same old tale, I suppose?"

"Yes," he said, "we've been very unlucky today, Mrs. Gubbins, very unlucky!"

"Unlucky! You always are unlucky," said the woman, bitterly.

"Can't help it," said the man, as he tossed the sixpence across the table. "That's every penny I got, Mrs. Gubbins, every penny."

"You ought to be ashamed of yourself, John Robinson," said the old woman, turning round at last, and glaring at him with her bloodshot eyes. "You ought to be ashamed of yourself, taking the bread out of your own bairns' mouths and a-giving of it to them as hasn't no sort of a claim upon you!"

"Not a word of that, mother," said the man. "It's of no use you saying aught about that. Haven't I told you so afore?"

"But I will say summat about it," said Mrs. Gubbins, "and I say it's a sin and a shame, it is; and what's more, I won't have it, I won't!"

"Hold your tongue," said the man, angrily, as he heard the sound of a little stifled sob from the corner of the room. "My Mary loved that bairn, and I'm not a-going to let her go."

"We'll see about that," said Mrs. Gubbins. "I'll have a word with the parish officer when I sees him next. What's the good of the House, I should like to know, if bairns as hasn't got nobody to look to 'em can't go there? I'll manage it, John Robinson, don't you be a-bothering of your head about it."

"But I tell you she shan't go!" said John, as he smote the table angrily. "I'll see *you* go first."

"Will you indeed?" said the woman, scornfully, as she covered herself with an old shawl, and laid down to sleep. "I'd like to see you, I would."

The man sat quite still, till the sound of her loud snoring broke the silence of the room. Then he crept to the corner where the children were sleeping. Faith was still awake, her hands were over her face, and she was crying quietly.

He bent over her and whispered softly, "Don't you take on so, little Faith; don't take no notice of her. They shan't *never* take you away from me, bless you! *Don't don't* cry, little Faith."

15

The child felt his hand on her hair stroking it very gently, and she felt something warm and wet fall on her hand! Could it be a tear?

2

Faith's Flight

*Y*es, it was a tear, and it was not the only tear which John Robinson shed that night. He loved little Faith dearly, quite as much as if she had been his own child. Her poor mother had died in the next attic when Faith was three weeks old. Her husband had deserted her some time before the baby was born, so that when she was gone the poor little thing was left alone in the world. John's wife, Mary, had brought it into their room, crying, cold, and hungry. She had comforted it, warmed it, and fed it, and they had never had the heart to turn it out again.

"Let her bide," Mary had said. "She'll, maybe, bring a blessing with her, poor bairn!"

And little Faith had been nothing but a blessing ever since—at least, so John Robinson thought. She had always loved him and always been a comfort to him. It was a year now since Mary had died, and Faith had been his little comforter ever since.

But what was to be done with the children whilst he and Faith were out on market days? That was the question to be decided when his wife died. And, in an evil moment, he had accepted the offer of his wife's mother, Mrs. Gubbins, to come and live with him, and to look after the little ones. He would never have had her if he had known what she was. But she lived in a town many miles away, and neither he nor Mary had seen her for many years. So when her letter came, in which she offered to come and live with him, he was very pleased, and thought it was a way out of his difficulty.

And Mrs. Gubbins came, and, having come, she stayed.

And in less than a week, his clean, comfortable room was changed into a pigsty. The children became neglected and disorderly, and all the quiet and peace and rest dropped out of his life.

But John Robinson was a weak man, and he became thoroughly afraid of Mrs. Gubbins. He had not the courage to send her away, and from day to day he endured in silence. He was cowed and unhappy; he longed to turn her out and dared not. But tonight she had roused his anger as never before. Send little Faith away! He would never allow her to do that! No, as soon as she woke, he would order her out and have his room in peace again. And with this resolution, John Robinson fell asleep.

But Faith was also making a resolution, and she did not go to sleep. She lay awake, listening intently to every sound in the room. Mrs. Gubbins was snoring loudly, and, after a time, John Robinson followed her example.

Faith listened a long time, to be quite sure he was asleep. Then she crept from under the blanket and stood upright on the floor. The boards creaked as she did this, and she stood perfectly still for some moments, that she might be sure that the noise had not awakened either the man or the old woman. But the snoring went on as before so Faith stooped down very, very quietly, and then she groped her way to the door.

It was quite dark, for the fire had gone out, and John Robinson had put out the candle before he went to sleep, and she was very much afraid of stumbling over Mrs. Gubbins, who was lying somewhere in front of the fire. Slowly and cautiously, and yet trembling so much that she could hardly stand, she felt her way to the door.

Oh, how the boards creaked and strained, and oh, how little Faith shook with fear!

But no one moved in the room! They did not hear the noise. John Robinson was tired out with his hard day's work, and Mrs. Gubbins was heavy with drink. It would have taken a much louder noise than little Faith's quiet footstep to have wakened either of them.

So Faith reached the door, quietly unlatched it, and crept out. Then she began to descend the long, rickety staircase. And this was a work of time, for it was almost impossible not to make some noise here, so rotten and broken were the boards. Oh, how thankful she felt when she had passed both the landings, and no one had heard her! And now she cautiously unbolted the street door and looked out.

It was a pitch-dark night—not a star was in the sky. The rain was falling fast, and by the light of the one dingy gaslight in the street, Faith could see that the road and pavement were covered with pools and mud. It was a dark, dismal, dreary night.

Little Faith was about to shut the door behind her and venture out into the darkness when she heard a footstep coming down the street. It came nearer and nearer. It was a man's footstep, and he was stumbling along as if he were drunk. Then he began to scream and to shout, and Faith drew back into the house and shut the door before he came up. She dared not venture into the darkness alone. She had heard that bad people were about at night. What if she should meet any of them?

No, she dared not go till the morning. She would sit on the stairs till it was light.

So, she crept back again, and sat on the lowest step, and leaned her head on her hands. The wind blew through the drafty old house and underneath the badly fitting door and made her shiver as she sat there. She was very cold, and very sad, and very tired.

But little Faith had a Friend. Yes, lonely and desolate as she was, she had a Friend to whom she could turn. He had been her Friend for a long time now, and as she sat there, alone in the darkness, she whispered softly to herself some words which Mother Mary, as she always called Mrs. Robinson, had taught her:

What a Friend we have in Jesus,
All our sins and griefs to bear;
What a privilege to carry
Everything to God in prayer!
Oh, what peace we often forfeit!
Oh, what needless pain we bear!
All because we do not carry
Everything to God in prayer.

Have we trials and temptations?
Is there trouble anywhere?
We should never be discouraged,
Take it to the Lord in prayer.

Can we find a friend so faithful,
Who will all our sorrows share?
Jesus knows our every weakness,
Take it to the Lord in prayer.

"Yes," she said, when she had finished the hymn. "I've never told Him nothing about it. Whatever will He think of me?"

So she knelt down on the step and said in a whisper, "God, I want to tell you, please, all about it. Mrs. Gubbins says I'm a-taking the bread out of the bairns' mouths, so please I'm a-going away, and will you help me to find somebody as wants a little servant? And will you please take care of Tommy, and Fanny, and the baby, and don't let Mrs. Gubbins slap 'em? For Jesus Christ's sake. Amen."

Then Faith got up and felt much happier. She knew her Friend would help her. She had carried it all to the Lord in prayer, and now she must not fret about it anymore. "That was what Mother Mary used to say," said Faith to herself. "She told me I was to take all my troubles to the Lord, and then leave 'em with Him, and not bother about 'em no more. She said it was a sin and a shame to doubt Him and to think He wouldn't give us aught, if we asked Him, and it was good for us."

So little Faith tried to forget her sorrow, and by and by she fell asleep. How long she slept she did not know, but when she awoke the grey morning light was creeping under the door, and peeping through the keyhole, and making the dirty, dusty walls of the old staircase visible once more.

Faith started up and opened the door and then went out into the rain and mud. It was still quite early. She had gone down several streets and felt as if she were a long way from home before the church clock struck five. The streets were almost empty. No one passed her except a solitary policeman, or a doctor returning from a patient who had sent for him in the night, or a workman whose work lay at a great distance from his home.

But presently, as time went on and it got near six o'clock, the streets were nearly filled with working men, in their white jackets, hurrying along to their work.

Then shutters began to be opened, and fires to be lighted, and smoke to come out of the chimneys.

Still Faith walked on. She wanted to get to quite a different part of that large town where nobody knew her and where she would never meet Mrs. Gubbins. She was very faint and hungry, for she had had no supper the night before. She had one penny in her pocket, which Mother Mary had given her long ago, and which she had kept for her sake. Faith had almost thought of giving it to her father, as she called John Robinson, the night before, when he was so unhappy about having taken so little money. But it would not have made much difference, and she was glad now that she had kept it, for it would buy her some breakfast. And then she must begin to look for a little place where she could be servant.

But, first, she must make herself tidy. No one would take an untidy little girl, she thought. For this purpose she went down an alley, where was a pump in the middle of the square, and washed her hands and her face. Then she took a comb from her pocket, which had belonged to the stall but which her father had given her the day before because it was broken and could not be sold. With this she combed her hair and plaited it neatly up again. Mary Robinson had taught her to be very clean and tidy, and her little frock, though it was full of patches and darns, had not a single hole in it. Since Mother Mary had died, Faith had mended it for herself. She looked a very clean, tidy child when she came out of the alley and set out in search of a

Faith makes herself tidy.

shop at which to spend her penny.

She found a baker's shop at last, but it was not open. The baker and his family had overslept themselves.

Faith was thinking of going on to look for another shop. But she turned so faint and sick that she was obliged to sit down on the baker's step. She felt she could walk no further until she had had something to eat.

At last the door was opened, and a boy came out and took down the shutters. Then Faith walked into the shop.

"Well what's wanted?" said the baker's daughter, as Faith held out the penny.

"Please," said Faith, in a faint voice, "I want the biggest cake you've got for a halfpenny."

"You look half hungered," said the girl, as she handed her a teacake. "Sit you down on that chair and eat it. Mother, come you here!" she called, in a louder voice.

A plump, rosy, good-tempered-looking woman answered the call.

"She wanted the biggest cake we've got for a halfpenny," said the girl. "Look at her; she's nigh hungered!"

"Where are you off to?" said the baker's wife to Faith, as she sat eating her cake.

"Please, ma'am," said little Faith, "I'm looking for a place. I'm going to be a little servant some-where. Do you know of anybody as wants a little girl?"

"Why, now," said the woman to her daughter, "doesn't Miss Benson want one?"

"Aye," said the girl, "so they say; but maybe she wouldn't take such as her."

"There's no harm in asking her, anyhow," said the baker's wife. "Take the child across to her, Maggie."

So Faith followed Maggie across the road. But, before she went, the good baker's wife gave her two more large teacakes and gave her the halfpenny back again which her daughter had taken.

"Jesus made her do that, I'm sure," said Faith to herself.

Miss Benson was not up, and they had to wait for some time to see her. Then, when she did come downstairs, she seemed quite angry with Faith for coming and with the baker's daughter for having brought her.

"Want a servant? Yes, she *did* want a servant; but a proper, respectable sort of servant, not a little, weakly, sickly child. She should have thought they would have known that, without needing to be told." And, so saying, she showed them out.

The baker's daughter took a kind leave of the child, but said she was afraid she did not know of anyone else.

So little Faith went on alone, very sorrowfully.

3

Faith's Search

*U*p and down the streets, up and down the streets, hour after hour, little Faith wandered, first asking at one shop and then at another. Sometimes she would venture to stop the passersby and inquire of them. She would choose someone whose face looked kind and motherly, and put the same question again and again: "Could you tell me of anyone as wants a little servant, please?"

But she got nothing but discouragement the whole day long. One told her that she was too small; another that she was too delicate; another brought tears to her eyes by telling her to go home to her mother; one or two laughed at her; and not a few were angry with her. And so the day wore away.

It was getting near evening and was beginning to grow dark. Faith had asked her question hopefully and eagerly in the morning; but now she asked it in quite a different voice, and as if she hardly expected an encouraging answer. She was very tired, and sad, and disappointed. Her Friend had not helped her, she thought. She had taken it to the Lord in prayer, but no answer had come. Mother Mary had said it was wicked to doubt, but how could she help doubting when God did not seem to hear her?

She was very footsore and tired, so she sat down on a doorstep to rest. She wondered very much what Mrs. Gubbins had said when she found she was gone; and whether her father missed her very much. She wondered whether he was looking for her all over that great town.

And then Faith remembered that it was Saturday night, and that her father would be at his place at the stall. She wondered how far the marketplace was from where she was sitting. She had a great longing just to see her father for a minute. She did not want him to see *her*—that would never do. No, she would never go home again till she had found a little place and was earning money for herself. But what she wanted was to try to get a peep at her father, to see if he looked sorrowful, or tired, or as if he were missing her very much.

Faith got up from the doorstep and asked a girl who was passing which was the way to the marketplace. The girl directed her and to Faith's joy she found it was close by.

In a few minutes she came in sight of the great church underneath the shadow of which stood John Robinson's stall. The street was very crowded; there was always a very full market on Saturday night. People were buying in their stores for the week and were going in and out of the different shops in the marketplace with large baskets on their arms. All was bustle, and hurry, and confusion.

Faith threaded her way through the crowd and went down a little side street which led into the marketplace and which ran along the side of the old church. She crept along close to the railings of the church, till she came nearly to the end of the street; but she did not dare to go further, lest her father should see her. She could see the top of the stall from where she stood, but she could not see her father. She did not like to go round the corner, for that would have brought her close up to the stall, and he would have seen her at once.

Faith had nearly made up her mind to go back again when she noticed that the church gate was open. She was almost afraid to go inside, but at last she ventured. In front of her was a porch leading into the church, and in this porch she saw that there was a window looking in the direction of the stall, through which she would be able to see her father without his seeing her. So she ran quickly across the open piece of churchyard and got inside the porch.

Then she looked out of the window. John Robinson's stall was not more than thirty yards away. She could see him quite well, surrounded as he was by flaring naphtha lights; but he could not see her at all in the darkness and shadow of the church porch.

This was just what little Faith wanted. She stood there for a long time watching him. He looked very sad, she thought, and very tired.

Nobody seemed to be buying anything, and she longed to run across the road and spend her penny at the stall. If only she could be somebody else, for just one moment, and run across and buy a penny toy, that he might have one more penny to take home to Mrs. Gubbins!

What would Mrs. Gubbins say if he brought her nothing home tonight? Well, there would be one mouth the less to feed, *that* was a comfort. She could not blame him anymore for giving the children's bread to her.

How anxiously Faith watched for customers to the stall, and how glad she was when at last an old man stopped and bought one of the best sixpenny pipes! But her father did not seem half as glad as she thought he would have been. He put the money in his pocket, but he did not look a bit pleased. He did not seem to be thinking much about it. All the time the old man was there, all the time he was showing off his wares, all the time he was waiting for purchasers, he was gazing up and down the street, first this way and then that way, as if he were looking for someone.

"Can he be looking for me?" said Faith to herself. "Oh, I hope he doesn't miss me so much!

P'raps I oughtn't never to have run away, but ought to have stopped with him and cheered him up. But I did it *all* for him. Mrs. Gubbins goes on at him so about me! Oh, dear, oh, dear; I hope he isn't very unhappy!"

There was a low stone seat on each side of the church porch, and Faith sat down on this and hid her face in her hands and cried. She was very tired and disheartened. Once she thought she would go out and go back to her father, but then she did not dare to go back to Mrs. Gubbins again till she had found a situation for herself. No, she could not do that.

But night was coming on and where should she sleep? She would be very frightened indeed if she had to be out alone in the street all night! What could she do? Should she pray again? She thought she would. Perhaps if she asked the Lord Jesus again to help her He would hear her. She could not understand why He had not heard her before. It was very strange! But she would try once more. She would tell Him how tired and lonely she was and how much she was afraid of being out in the street all night. Perhaps when He saw how very unhappy she was, He would tell her where to go.

Faith peeps into the church.

Faith was just going to kneel down when she heard the sound of singing inside the church. She put her ear to the door and listened.

Faith thought she had never heard such a beautiful tune. She opened the door just a little crack, that she might, if possible, hear the words. Then she peeped in. To her astonishment she could not see anyone in the church. One or two of the gas lamps were lighted, and she could see the great stone pillars and the high arches and long aisles of the old church, but she could not see a single man or woman or child. There were a great many pews, but they were all empty; and there was a high pulpit, but no one was standing in it. She opened the door a little wider and went in. There did not seem to be anyone in the old church but herself.

Where could the singing have come from?

Faith walked a few steps farther into the church and then she stopped again. She felt rather afraid at the sound of her feet upon the stone pavement. The singing had stopped, but presently she heard the voice of someone reading aloud. The voice seemed to come from the other side of the church. After waiting for some minutes, Faith walked on tiptoe in that direction. She wanted very much to know from whence the sound came.

Presently she saw a door in that part of the church open, and an old man looked out to see who was walking about in the church. He caught sight of Faith and came towards her. She felt very much inclined to run away; she was afraid he would be angry with her for coming into the church.

But the old man did not look cross or vexed, but smiled at her as he came up, so Faith settled not to run away.

When the old man was close to her he asked her, in a whisper, what she wanted.

"Please, sir," said Faith, "I wanted to hear 'em sing; they was singing so beautifully when I was outside there—but I couldn't find nobody!"

"They're all in the vestry," said the old verger. "It's prayer meeting night. It's always prayer meeting of a Saturday night. You'll have to sit very still if I let you come in."

"Will they let me in?" said Faith, in a faltering voice. "Won't they be cross if I go?"

"Oh, no," said the man, "not if I take you, bairn, and if you are a good girl. Come along; you can sit on the seat by me." So he gave Faith his hand and took her into the vestry.

The vestry was nearly full. There were about thirty people present, sitting in rows, and the minister was standing in front of them, reading a chapter out of the Bible. Then they knelt down and prayed.

Little Faith was very tired and sleepy. She sat in the corner by the old verger, and he kept nodding kindly to her. But the warmth and comfort of the room, after her bad night, and after the cold and fatigue of the day, made her eyes very heavy.

Presently, as the minister was reading again, she fell asleep. She had not been asleep more than a minute or two when she was wakened up suddenly by hearing her own name. She had been dreaming of Mother Mary and thought she was sitting beside Mother Mary's bed, as she had done for so many days and nights before she died. And then she thought someone asked her a question, and this question awoke her: "Little Faith, wherefore didst thou doubt?"

She started up and opened her eyes, but Mother Mary was not there! Faith found herself in the vestry on the seat beside the old man. He looked very surprised to see her jump up so suddenly.

And yet she felt quite sure that she had really heard a voice asking her that question. Yes, and she felt quite sure that it was the same voice which was reading now! It was the minister who had said: "Little Faith, wherefore didst thou doubt?"

How could he know about her? Who could have told him that her name was little Faith? How did he know that she had been praying, and had not got an answer to her prayer, and was beginning to doubt?

Jesus must have told him; she felt sure of that. Nobody else knew.

The minister did not say anything more about her. She listened very attentively now, but he did not mention her name again. He was reading about a ship, and the wind ceasing, and the ship getting to land.

It was very strange that he should have stopped in the middle to speak to her! But little Faith felt she had got a message from heaven. Jesus must have told him to ask her that question. He was very sorry she had doubted Him and told the minister to tell her so.

Faith said to herself that she would never doubt anymore. She was quite sure now that she would have an answer to her prayer very soon indeed. Her Friend had heard her after all and was going to help her. She felt quite glad and happy, and as if a great weight had been taken off her heart.

4

A Happy Sunday

The prayer was over, the blessing was given, and the people rose to leave. But little Faith still sat on. The old verger came up to her and told her kindly that it was all done now and she had better be thinking of going home, as it was getting late, and he was going to lock the church up.

"Please, sir," said little Faith, "do you think the minister would let me speak to him?"

"Aye, to be sure," said the old man. "Wait a minute and I'll ask him."

The minister was talking to an old lady, who had stopped behind the rest to tell him of someone who was ill and wanted to see him. As soon as she had done speaking, the verger went up to him, and, pointing to Faith, said, "Here's a little girl as has been sitting by me in the meeting, wants to speak to you, sir."

The minister called Faith to him and asked her what she wanted.

"Please, sir," said the child, "I won't never do it again."

"You won't do what, my child?" said the minister.

"I won't never doubt Him again," said little Faith. "It was very wrong, I know it was—Mother Mary said so; but I won't do it no more, I won't. Did He tell you to speak to me and to ask me that?"

The minister looked very puzzled.

"What does she mean, Barnes?" he said to the old verger. "When did I speak to her and ask her anything? I cannot remember that I ever saw her before."

"Please, sir," said Faith, "it was just now when I was a-sitting there by him. I was very tired with walking about all day, and I was very nigh asleep, and then I heard you calling of me, and asking that."

"I think you must have been dreaming, dear child," said the minister. "I never asked you anything."

"Didn't you?" said little Faith, in a very disappointed voice. "Oh! I thought it was you; it must have been a dream, then!"

"What was it, dear?" said the old lady, who had been putting on her cloak whilst they were talking. "What did you think Mr. Barker asked you?"

"Please, ma'am," said Faith, with tears in her eyes, "I heard somebody saying to me, 'Little Faith, wherefore didst thou doubt?' and I thought it was the minister and that Jesus had told him what they called me and all about me."

"Oh, I see now, I think," said the minister kindly. "Is your name Faith?"

"Yes, sir," said the child. "Faith Emmerson."

"It was in the chapter I read tonight," said Mr. Barker to the old lady. "Don't you remember Jesus said to Peter, 'O thou of little faith, wherefore didst thou doubt?'"

"Yes, of course!" said the old lady. "That was it. Poor child! Wasn't it strange?"

"Then Jesus didn't tell you about me, after all?" said the child.

44

"No," said Mr. Barker. "He did not tell me about you. But I am sure, if you have been doubting Him, little Faith, that He has sent you here that I might ask you that question. I am quite sure He meant it for you. Now will you not tell me why you have been doubting Him? What was it about?"

Little Faith burst into tears. "Oh, please," she said. "Mrs. Gubbins says I'm taking bread out of the children's mouths, so I've run away to be a little servant; and nobody wants me. I walked about all day asking of people, and there isn't nobody as wants me. I've asked at all the little shops, and none of 'em wants a girl just now; and I've asked the folks in the street, and none of 'em wanted anybody neither. There isn't nobody wants me! And afore I started I asked Jesus to help me, and He hasn't helped me a bit yet, and now I don't know whatever I shall do tonight!"

"Now," said the minister, "I want to hear all about it. Sit down on the seat beside me and tell me. And first, who is Mrs. Gubbins?"

Little Faith sat down beside the minister, and little by little he got from her her history; and when she had told him all, and he understood quite well what she wanted, he turned to the old lady, who was waiting and listening also, and asked her advice as to what was to be done.

"Don't you think you had better go home to your father tonight, Faith, and stop with him till I hear of a situation for you?" said the old lady.

"Oh, please not," said Faith. "I don't want never to go back to Mrs. Gubbins again. What would she say? She'd maybe be ever so angry with me. Oh, please don't send me back till I can tell them I've got a little place!"

"Well, Mr. Barker," said the old lady, after thinking for a minute or two, "I'll take little Faith home with me tonight. She may stop with me till Monday, and then we can talk about it again and see what can be done."

"That is indeed good of you, Mrs. Fraser," said the minister. "Little Faith, Jesus has heard your prayer, you see, and has sent this kind lady to help you."

Little Faith was smiling very happily now, poor child. She felt as if the burden had been rolled away from her.

They went out of the vestry and walked through the old church, where Barnes was busy putting out the gaslights. Then they came to the church porch, and Faith could see her father. He was still standing behind the stall, holding up his wares to the passersby.

"Please, ma'am," said Faith to the old lady, "that's my father."

"Had not we better go and tell him, Faith?" she said.

"No, please not," said little Faith, "not till I've got a little place. Please don't tell him now."

So when they got to the gate the old lady and Faith went the other way round the church. The minister said, "Good-night," for he was going to see the sick person of whom Mrs. Fraser had told him.

Mrs. Fraser took hold of Faith's hand, and they went on down several streets till they came to the old lady's house. They stopped before the door, and Mrs. Fraser rang the bell. It was not at all a large house, but it looked very grand and beautiful to little Faith. There was a small bow window on one side of the door. The venetian blinds were down but not closed, and the flickering of the firelight within looked very comfortable and inviting.

The door was opened by a clean, tidy servant, in a white muslin apron and white cap.

"Now, Ellen," said her mistress, "I've brought this little girl to spend Sunday here. Will you give her some tea and take care of her? Now, Faith, go with Ellen; I am sure you will be happy with her."

Faith followed Ellen into the cozy little kitchen, where there was a blazing fire; and Ellen told her to sit down on a stool in front of the fire, whilst she got her mistress's supper ready.

Faith sat still and watched Ellen moving about the kitchen, quickly and yet quietly, and setting out the supper tray very neatly and prettily; and she wondered if ever she would be so clever and be able to be of so much use as a servant.

Then the tray was carried into the room, and Ellen came back to attend to Faith. She made the child take off her wet frock, and she brought down a warm jacket of her own for Faith to wear till her frock was dry. And then she gave her such a supper as Faith had not had for many a day, certainly not since Mother Mary died. The food and the hot coffee brought a color into her pale cheeks, and Ellen declared she looked "a sight better now."

Faith was very glad to go to bed and slept very soundly after her long, tiring day.

The next day was Sunday, and what a happy Sunday it was for Faith! She went with Ellen to the old church, and sat beside her, and heard the minister preach and the people sing. She thought it must be very like that in heaven where Mother Mary was.

Then, after tea, she and Ellen went into the dining room to old Mrs. Fraser, and they read a chapter together in the Bible, and the old lady talked to them about it. Faith could read a little. She had always gone to school when Mother Mary was alive, except on market days, and then her father had her read to him as they sat together on the box behind the stall. Faith was very pleased to be allowed to read her verse in turn.

Mrs. Fraser chose the chapter which the minister had read at the prayer meeting on Saturday night, and in which came the question which Faith had heard as she woke up from sleep: "O thou of little faith, wherefore didst thou doubt?"

"Do you love the Lord Jesus, little Faith?" said Mrs. Fraser, when she had done reading.

"Yes, ma'am," said little Faith, "ever so much, I do."

"Why do you love Him, Faith?" asked the old lady.

"Please, ma'am, because He died for me. Mother Mary said I couldn't never go to heaven if Jesus hadn't died for me. She said God would have had to have punished me for being naughty so often and couldn't never have taken me to live in His beautiful home, if Jesus hadn't been punished 'stead of me. It *was* good of Him, it was!"

"I am *so* glad you know that," said the old lady, "because we have no right to call God our Friend, little Faith, till we have come to Jesus as our Savior. Many people talk about God helping them, and God being merciful to them, and yet all the time they never come to God through Jesus, never take Jesus for their *own* Savior. But you *have* done that, haven't you, little Faith?"

"Yes, please, ma'am," said little Faith. "Mother Mary taught me a hymn, to say when I said my prayers of a night and morning. It begins:

Just as I am—without one plea,
But that Thy blood was shed for me,

And that Thou bidst me come to Thee,
O Lamb of God, I come.

And I try to come every time I say it."

"Dear child," said Mrs. Fraser, "I am so glad of that. And now, little Faith, I am sure you *have* a Friend in Jesus, and so you must never doubt Him, little Faith. 'Wherefore didst thou doubt?' Don't forget that question; it grieves Him so if you doubt Him."

"Yes," said little Faith, "Mother Mary said so."

"Just think, Faith," said the old lady, "after I've tried to be kind to you, and taken you in here, and am trying to make you happy, and am ready to do anything I can for you, if you were to doubt *me* and to say: 'I don't think Mrs. Fraser will give me any breakfast tomorrow,' or 'I don't think Mrs. Fraser will really look out for a place for me,' and 'I don't believe this,' or 'I'm so afraid of that,' why, little Faith, what *should* I think of you?"

Little Faith laughed.

"I wouldn't *never* do that," she said.

"No, little Faith," said the old lady, "you wouldn't doubt me. Then, do you think you ought to doubt the Lord Jesus, who has done so much more for you than I have done?"

"No," said Faith, "I must never do it again."

Then Mrs. Fraser knelt down and prayed that she and Ellen and Faith might always trust their heavenly Friend and never doubt His love, but that every time they felt tempted to do so, they might hear His tender, loving voice saying to them as He did to Peter, "O thou of little faith, wherefore didst thou doubt?"

5

The Empty Place

It was Friday morning, and little Faith was going to the market to see her father. She had waited until Friday that she might be able to see him at the stall, for she did not want to go home to meet Mrs. Gubbins.

Faith had so much to tell her father that he would be pleased to hear. The minister and Mrs. Fraser had had a long talk about her on Tuesday evening, and it had been settled that they should get her father's consent for her to stop in Mrs. Fraser's house for six months. During that time, the old lady and Ellen would teach her and train her to be a useful little servant, and then the minister and Mrs. Fraser very kindly promised to find a nice situation for her, where she might earn money for herself. Oh how glad her father would be when he heard this good news!

Faith dressed herself very tidily, in the pretty pink frock which Mrs. Fraser and Ellen had made for her, and put on her new brown hat, trimmed so prettily and so neatly with brown velvet. "I wonder if father will know me?" said Faith to herself, as she looked in the looking glass before starting. "Maybe he'll think it's somebody else. He'll never think it's me, as smart as this! Oh dear, how pleased he'll be!"

It was quite early when Faith started for the marketplace, not more than nine o'clock. She was so happy that Friday morning that she hardly knew what she was doing. She had helped Ellen to get the breakfast ready, but she had spilled the milk and let the kettle boil over, and had let one of the silver spoons fall, and had had so many mishaps in various ways, that Ellen had laughed at her and had told her that she had better get her breakfast and go at once, for it was clear she was too excited to do anything else.

So now Faith was ready to go. She ran quickly downstairs, and in the hall she found Mrs. Fraser.

"Well, little Faith," said the old lady, "tell your father I will take great care of you—and take this with you to spend at the stall. You will like to buy something, I know." And Mrs. Fraser put a florin into the child's hand and told her that she might buy anything she pleased with it.

Two shillings to spend at her father's stall!

If Faith had been in good spirits before, she was almost wild now. Two shillings! What a number of things that would buy! And her father, how pleased he would be! No one had ever spent two shillings at the stall before. Mrs. Gubbins would be almost in a good temper if he took so much money home to her at night.

What should she buy? She thought she would get a nice present for Ellen, who had been so kind to her. What should it be? She turned over in her mind all the contents of the stall but could not fix upon anything. No, she must wait until she got there and talk it over with her father.

Oh how surprised he would be when she appeared and how glad and thankful when he heard how happy she was and how good God had been to her! Faith felt as if her feet would not go fast enough. It seemed such a long time since she had seen her father, and it was almost like a dream to think of speaking to him again and telling him of all that had happened to her during that strange week.

At last the old church came in sight, and Faith turned down the little side street that she might come out just in front of her father's stall. She was getting very near now; she could see the basket stall and the cap stall, which were just at the end of the street. Another moment and she would be there! Oh, how little Faith's heart beat as she hurried on!

She turned the corner—and then she suddenly stood still—rooted to the spot in amazement and dismay. Her father was not there! The stocking stall, the gingerbread stall, the bootlace stall, and all the other toy stalls were going on as usual, but her father's place was empty.

Little Faith was so disappointed that she burst into tears.

What could be the reason? Where could her father be? Had he changed his place? She wandered a little way down the marketplace to see, but no—that was not likely, for she had often heard him say that he liked this place at the corner of the two streets better than any in the market-place.

And then, too, her father's place was empty, no other stall had been moved there.

What could be the matter? She was sure that no small reason would keep him away from the stall. She could only remember one market day when he had not been there, and that was the day Mother Mary had died. That sorrowful day! It was very fresh in little Faith's memory still. She remembered how they sat by her bed and her father was holding her hand, and she had said, "You won't go today, John," and he had said, "No, dear, of course I won't." And then he had sat there, holding her hand, till she had gone away from them to heaven.

Little Faith had thought of all this now, as she sat down on the copingstone of the church rail-ings, wondering what had become of her father. What could be the matter? Was one of the chil-dren dead? Had Mrs. Gubbins been getting drunk and let them fall into the fire or down the stairs? Little Faith had always been afraid of that and had always charged Tommy, the eldest one, to take care of the others whilst she was out. Could it be that? It made her shudder to think of it! Or was her father ill—very, very ill, like Mother Mary had been, with no one to nurse him, or love him, or look after him? It was a dreadful thought, and the tears ran down the child's face as her mind dwelt upon it.

Suddenly it occurred to her that she would ask the other stall keepers if they had seen anything of her father. So she went up to Tom Jenkins, the owner of the basket stall, and asked him if he had seen her father in the marketplace that morning.

"Why, bless me!" said Jenkins, looking very closely at her. "Is it little Faith?"

"Yes," said Faith. "It's me. I've got a little place. I came to tell father about it, and he's gone."

"Well," said Jenkins, "I can't think, for the life of me, what's got him. He was here on Tuesday, only half the day, though. But he hasn't been here today."

"Did he look ill?" said little Faith.

"Aye," said Jenkins, "very downhearted, he did. I don't know what was wrong with him. I said to my mate there, when we went home at night, says I, 'There must be something amiss with Robinson.' But he never said nothing about it to none of us."

"What can it be?" said little Faith.

"I don't know, my lass, I'm sure," said the basket man, as he turned away to show off his wares to some country people who were passing the stall. "Maybe yon man yonder will know," and he pointed to the cap stall proprietor, who was standing idly behind his stall with his hands in his pockets.

Faith went to him, but he could give her no information whatever. She asked at one or two of the other stalls, but with the same result. No one could throw the least light on the reason of her father's absence. There was nothing to be done but to go back and tell Mrs. Fraser.

So with a heavy heart Faith turned back. How slowly she walked homewards, so differently from the way in which she had come down to the marketplace. She even turned round once or twice and looked at the empty place again, as if it could not possibly be anything but a dream that her father's stall had vanished from the place where it had stood so long.

When Faith got to the house, Ellen let her in and was beginning to ask her, in a cheerful voice, if her father knew her, when she noticed how sad and downcast the child looked.

"Where is Mrs. Fraser?" said little Faith, as she began to cry again.

"She's here in the dining room," said Ellen, kindly. "Come in and speak to her."

She opened the door, and Faith went in. Holding out the florin she sobbed out, "Please, ma'am, he's gone; he isn't there! I can't find him nowheres! None of the stall keepers has seen him today. Oh, dear, whatever shall I do?"

Mrs. Fraser made Faith sit down beside her and talked it over with her for a long time. At last it was decided that, after dinner, Faith should go to her old home to see what was the matter there.

Faith did not eat much dinner that day. She was very anxious and very troubled. She did not forget, before she started, to go into the little bedroom which she shared with Ellen, and, kneeling down, take her trouble to the Lord in prayer, asking her heavenly Friend to go with her. For she could not help dreading meeting Mrs. Gubbins again, and she did not know in what trouble or sorrow she might find her father. As she went down the well-known streets and got nearer and nearer to Belfry Row, she kept asking again and again for help for whatever was before her.

At last little Faith reached the house and quietly opened the door. And then she stood still and felt almost afraid to go farther.

What would Mrs. Gubbins say when she went in? All Faith's dread of the old woman returned upon her.

She crept cautiously and quietly up the rickety stairs. The house was very noisy, as usual. The two landings were full of screaming, quarreling children, and bad and angry words were heard on all sides. Faith had never noticed how wretched the house looked before. When she had lived there, she was so accustomed to the noise and the dirt and the misery that she had hardly seen it.

But now, coming from Mrs. Fraser's beautiful house, where everything was so clean and comfortable, Faith wondered how she could ever have been happy in Belfry Row. It looked so very forlorn and wretched, she thought.

The people on the two landings took no notice of her as she passed by. John Robinson's family had kept very much to themselves and did not know any of the other people in the house. There was no one now living on the same floor with them, and those below seemed as far away as if they lived in another house, for they never saw them except when they passed by their rooms as they went down to the street door. They did not even know their names. The people of the house were constantly changing; nearly every week fresh ones came. So, even if they had wished to get to know them, it would have been very difficult. So Faith passed by, and no one stopped her or noticed her.

At last she reached the top landing, and there before her was the well-known door. She waited for a minute or two, wondering what she should do, and then she knocked.

No one came to open the door, and Faith could not hear any sound inside the room. Surely the children could not be asleep yet; it was only four o'clock. The church clock in the street struck as she stood at the door.

Faith knocked again and waited again but she got no answer. "They must be all out," she thought. "I expect the door is locked; I shall have to come again." She wondered where they could have gone. They had never all been out together since Mother Mary died.

Faith thought she would try the door before she went away. Perhaps Mrs. Gubbins had been looking out of the window, and would not let her in, and was making the children sit very quiet that she might not hear them.

Faith's heart beat very fast at the thought. Should she lift the latch and go in? What would Mrs. Gubbins do? Would she knock her down as soon as she went in and then turn her out? Not if her father were there, Faith felt sure of that. But she did not think her father *could* be there, unless he was very ill, or he would have opened the door.

No, they must all be out. She would just try the door and then go away.

So Faith put her hand on the latch and was almost startled at the sound it made going down.

The door was open, and Faith went in.

6

What Faith Found
in the Attic

𝒯aith went into the room, but it was not empty.
Her father was not there, nor the children, but in
the corner of the room, in the place where the children used to sleep, Mrs. Gubbins was lying on the
ground with her face turned to the wall. She did
not look round as Faith went in, but lay perfectly
still.

Could she be asleep, or was she only pretending
to be asleep, that Faith might go away again? The
child felt tempted to do this; she was so terrified
at the thought of being alone there with Mrs.
Gubbins. But then she remembered that it was

almost teatime. Surely her father and the children would soon be in, and then she could see them before she went.

So Faith sat down on a box and waited. Mrs. Gubbins did not move nor speak, and Faith concluded that she must really be asleep. No doubt she had been drinking heavily and had fallen on the bed to sleep the heavy sleep of drunkenness, as Faith had seen her do so often before. On the table was a black bottle and a broken cup. The bottle had no cork in it and was lying on its side. There was a strong smell of spirits in the room, as if the old woman had knocked it over when she got up from her seat, and the contents had been spilled on the floor.

Faith sat still on the box, straining her ears for the sound of her father's footstep on the stairs; but no one came. Not a sound broke the silence, except the distant noise of quarreling and screaming children which came up from below.

The room was very cold. The fire had evidently burnt out some time since, and Faith shivered as she sat near the door. She once thought that she would go farther into the room where she would be out of the way of the draft; but she was so much afraid that Mrs. Gubbins would wake and be angry with her, that she thought she would keep close to the door, that she might make her escape as soon as the old woman moved.

Time passed on, and still no one came.

What could they be doing? Where could her father have taken them?

The church clock struck five. It was getting dark now. Faith could only dimly see the form of Mrs. Gubbins stretched in the corner of the attic. She did not know what to do. Mrs. Fraser would be expecting her at home and would wonder that she had stayed so long, and yet she could not bear the thought of not seeing her father after all. Was there no one who could tell her anything about him. No, she could not think of anyone. The people downstairs were newcomers and probably did not know anything whatever of the inhabitants of the attic. There was no one but Mrs. Gubbins. Should she awake her and ask her, or should she go away without hearing of her father.

Faith decided to go away, but when she was halfway down the stairs she changed her mind. It would be terrible to wait till tomorrow to know what was the matter with her father. All night long she would be wondering where he was, and she would lie awake thinking of him, she was sure of that. For a very dreadful thought had crossed her mind. Was her father dead, and had Mrs. Gubbins sent the children to the workhouse? The more Faith thought of this, the more she felt afraid that this was what was the matter. She could not go home without knowing the truth. So she went back again and knocked once more, very loudly, at the attic door. She hoped that Mrs. Gubbins would awake and come to the door, and then she could speak to her there without going inside.

But no sound was to be heard within, though Faith repeated her knock three or four times. So she opened the door and went into the attic again. Mrs. Gubbins was lying just as Faith had seen her before. She did not seem to have moved at all.

"I shall have to speak to her," said the child to herself. "She seems so very sound asleep."

She crossed the rotten floor, trembling at the noise she made, and went up to where Mrs. Gubbins was lying.

Then Faith stood still for a minute and prayed. She took it to the Lord in prayer. She asked her Friend to stand by her, and help her, and not to let

Mrs. Gubbins hurt her.

As she prayed, she happened to look up at the skylight window, and there, looking down into the dark, dismal attic, was a bright and beautiful star. Little Faith looked at the star, and it seemed to be smiling at her, she thought. It seemed like the loving eye of the Lord Jesus watching her, and she thought she heard Him asking her that question again, "Little Faith, wherefore didst thou doubt?"

Oh, what strength it gave her! Faith felt that her prayer was heard. Jesus was by her side, and He would help her. She would be no longer afraid.

"Mrs. Gubbins!" said Faith, in a whisper. "Mrs. Gubbins!"

But Mrs. Gubbins did not hear.

"Mrs. Gubbins! Mrs. Gubbins!" she repeated, much louder than before.

But no answer came.

"Mrs. Gubbins! Mrs. Gubbins!" She almost shouted the words this time, but still the old woman did not move. "How very sound asleep she must be!" thought the child.

It was nearly dark now, so that Faith could only just see Mrs. Gubbins' face, but she fancied that her eyes were not quite closed. One hand was hanging out from under the blanket close to Faith, and the child took hold of it, thinking that she would in this way be able to arouse the old woman from her heavy sleep.

But she had no sooner taken Mrs. Gubbins' hand than she started back in terror. The hand was icy cold. Faith had never felt anything like it since Mother Mary died. She remembered how she had crept to Mother Mary's side the night after she died, not liking to go to sleep without giving her a kiss as usual, and then she remembered how startled she had been to find her so very very cold, for she had never seen death before. And now Mrs. Gubbins' hand felt just like that, just as cold, just as motionless. Could Mrs. Gubbins be dead?

Faith ran to the door and down the stairs as fast as she could.

"What is it? What's the matter?" said a woman who was coming out of her room on the next landing, and heard Faith's footstep, and saw by the light of her candle how pale and frightened the child looked.

"Oh, please," said little Faith. "I wish you'd come upstairs; I believe she's dead!"

"Dead! Who's dead?" said the woman. "What is it, child? Tell me who's dead!"

"Mrs. Gubbins!" said Faith. "The old woman as lives upstairs. Haven't you never seen her passing by?"

"What? That old woman as is always going out for drink? Aye, I've seen her," said the woman.

Two or three more women came out of their rooms at this moment, and they all agreed to go upstairs with Faith.

The woman with the candle went first and flashed the light on the old woman's face.

"Yes, she's gone," she said, solemnly. "She's gone, poor thing! Dear me, has she never anybody belonging to her?"

Faith told them in a few words who she was, and asked them if they could tell her anything of her father and the children. One woman told her that they had left the house together last Tuesday afternoon and had never been seen since. But where they had gone no one knew. Another woman said Mrs. Gubbins had been backwards and forwards several times the day before with a bottle in her hand, but none of them had seen her at all today.

Then they talked together about what was to be done. The news had by this time spread all over the house and throughout Belfry Row, and quite a crowd of people filled the little attic—mothers with babies in their arms, troops of noisy, dirty children, and one or two idle and ragged men.

After much talking and after many exclamations of horror, and after each person had separately related when was the last time that he or she had seen Mrs. Gubbins, and when they had also all related, in turn, what had been the exact state of their feelings of horror and surprise when they had been summoned to the attic just now, and had been told that she was dead—they came to the conclusion that Jem Payne, one of their number, should go at once to the parish officer and report the case to him and leave all further steps in the matter in his hands.

When all this was settled, Faith turned to go. She was very glad to be able to leave the attic and go homewards. She felt very awestruck and solemn as she walked home, and yet she could hardly realize it. Mrs. Gubbins dead! Alone in the attic dead! And her father gone she knew not where! It all seemed too strange and too dreadful to be true.

Faith was very glad when she reached Mrs. Fraser's house and was able to tell the kind old lady all that had happened.

"Oh, Faith!" said Mrs. Fraser, when she had heard it all and they were talking it over together. "May God keep you, my dear child, from the love of drink! It is a terrible thing when a man drinks, but oh, I think it is worse when a woman drinks!"

"Mrs. Gubbins didn't always drink so bad," said Faith. "But she got worse and worse lately."

"Yes," said Mrs. Fraser, "people always get worse and worse. Satan tempts them, and then they yield. Then he tempts them again, and they yield again, and he gets a greater hold on them every time. Only God's grace, little Faith, can enable a drunkard to lose his love for drink; nothing else will do it. Pledges alone cannot do it; resolutions alone cannot do it; nothing but God's grace helping him can keep him from falling. Does your father drink, little Faith?"

"Oh, no," said Faith. "*Never*—not a drop, he doesn't. He always brought every penny he took home to Mother Mary, and then, when she was dead, to Mrs. Gubbins. Oh, poor father, I wonder where he is!"

"Do you remember that verse, Faith," said Mrs. Fraser, "'If ye shall ask anything in My name, I will do it'?"

The child thought she had heard it before, but she did not know it perfectly, so Mrs. Fraser found it for her in her Testament and made her learn it.

"Now, little Faith," she said, when the child had repeated the verse correctly, "God knows where your father is. He sees him at this moment, just as you see me. He sees what he is doing, and what the children are doing. He knows the name of the place they are in, and the name of the street, and the number of the house. He knows all about them, whether they are ill or well, or in want or comfort. Now, little Faith, you would like very much to know about all this too, wouldn't you?"

"Oh, yes," said little Faith, "that I should, ma'am!"

"Very well," said Mrs. Fraser, "then we will kneel down and ask God to tell you, and then, if it is good for you to know, I am quite sure, little Faith, that in some way or other He will help you. Little Faith, can you believe that?"

"Yes," said the child. "I think I can."

So Mrs. Fraser and Faith knelt down together.

It was a very simple prayer, so simple that Faith could understand every word of it. Mrs. Fraser took all the trouble to the Lord in prayer, telling Him the sorrow of little Faith's heart, and how she longed to know where her father was, and asking Him, if He saw it would be good for her, to let her know.

"Now, Faith," said Mrs. Fraser, when they rose from their knees, "having done this you must leave the matter with God, who knows best. Do not trouble about it anymore, because, if you do that, you will show plainly that you do not trust Him. Go about your work patiently, and, whenever you are tempted to be sorrowful, you must think that you hear the Lord Jesus saying to you, 'O thou of little faith, wherefore didst thou doubt?' If you only trust Him, really trust Him, an answer will come. I am sure of that."

Little Faith wiped away her tears and went downstairs with a bright and cheerful face. She had taken her trouble to the Lord in prayer, and she had left it with Him.

Now she had nothing to do but to wait patiently for the answer.

7

Found at Last

$\mathcal{I}$t is never easy to be patient. As days and weeks and even months went by, and Faith heard nothing of her father, sometimes her faith failed her. She wondered if, after all, God would answer her prayer. But Mrs. Fraser always cheered her, and encouraged her, and told her she must be willing to wait God's time.

The child was very happy in Mrs. Fraser's house, and day by day she was becoming more useful as a servant. Ellen had great pleasure in teaching her to do all kinds of housework and in training her in habits of neatness and order.

The six months during which Mrs. Fraser had promised to keep her were almost ended, but the old lady did not seem at all inclined to look out for a situation for Faith. She told the minister that the child was too young to go amongst strangers and to do hard work and that she would like to keep her in her own house, to pay her wages, and to train her until she was older and stronger. Faith was very thankful when she heard of this kind offer, for she was quite sure that she would never be so happy anywhere as she was in Mrs. Fraser's house. All went on so peacefully and happily there from day to day. The mistress was thoughtful and considerate for the comfort of her servants, and the servants loved their kind mistress and would not have grieved her for the world. Every morning and night they prayed together and took their wants, and sins, and sorrows, to the Lord in prayer.

Ellen found in Faith a very willing little helper in her work. She never idled away her time but did her work cheerfully and well. When she was sent on an errand, she went as quickly as she could and never stopped to talk or gossip on the way.

One bright September morning, just six months after Faith had come to live with Mrs.

Fraser, Ellen sent her to a shop at some little distance from home to buy something that was needed for dinner.

It so happened that, in order to get to this shop, Faith had to pass down the marketplace. It was so strange to see everything there looking just the same as it did in the days when she and her father used to stand behind the toy stall three times a week. The country people were hurrying past as usual; the sweets stall and the gingerbread stall were still surrounded by children; the stocking man, the bootlace man, and the basket man were still loudly calling to the passersby to come and examine their wares.

Faith stopped for a moment before the place where her father's stall had stood. A new toy stall was there in its place, and a man was standing behind it, and his little girl was helping him to sell his goods, just as she had always helped her father

"I wonder if they have taken much today?" said Faith to herself.

The little girl looked pale and tired, she thought, and the man did not seem to be in very good spirits.

Faith had sixpence of her own in her pocket, and she determined to spend it at the stall. Perhaps they would be as glad as she and her father would have been on one of those long, tiring days which now seemed so far away. So she went up to the stall and bought a new sixpenny comb.

The little girl smiled and seemed so pleased to get the sixpence, that Faith went on with a light and happy heart.

She had nearly passed the old church when she heard someone calling her. Looking round, she saw the owner of the basket stall waving his arms and calling "Faith!" at the top of his voice. She ran to him at once to see what he wanted.

"Here, my lass," said the man, "have you ever heard aught of your father?"

"No," said little Faith, "not a word."

"Well," said he, "my Matty said she saw him go by the other day."

"Oh, where?" cried little Faith. "Where did she see him? Was it here?"

"Oh, no," said the man, as he wiped his eyes with the back of his hand. "Matty won't never come here no more; you remember Matty, don't you?"

"Is she your little girl that used to come with you?" said Faith.

"Aye," he said, "the same; but she's very badly now. She'll never come no more, so the doctor says!"

"I'm so sorry," said little Faith.

"Would you mind telling me where she saw my father?"

"She saw him pass the window. I was out at the stall, but when I came in, 'Father,' she says, 'I saw the toy stall man, who used to be next to us, go by today; he must live somewheres here.' She never forgets folks' faces, doesn't Matty. Go and see her. She'll tell you all about it."

He told Faith where he lived, and then she hurried on to make up for lost time.

Was her prayer really going to be answered at last? It was a very happy thought, and it was with a very bright face that she carried the good news to Mrs. Fraser. The old lady was very glad to hear it, though she told Faith not to be too sure that by this means she should find her father but to believe that even if it did not come now, still God's answer to her prayer would not stop away a single day after God's time came.

That afternoon Mrs. Fraser gave Faith leave to go to Trundle Street, where little Matty lived, that she might hear all that the child could tell her.

It was a dark, dismal street, full of high houses let off in rooms, and was very much like Belfry Row, Faith's old home. The room to which the basket man had directed her to go was on the ground floor, on the left-hand side of the door.

Faith knocked gently, and a voice within said: "Come in; they are all out but me."

So Faith opened the door and went in. It was a low, dark room, and, at first, Faith could hardly see who or what was in it. There was not much furniture, but the room was almost filled with baskets of various sizes and shapes and colors, so that there was very little space to move about in it.

On a bed, close to the window, a little girl was lying. She was propped up with pillows, so that she could see what was passing in the street. She was about Faith's age, or a little older, but she was so very thin and small that Faith could easily have carried her. When the door was first opened she coughed very much and seemed in much pain.

"Why, it's Faith," she said, as soon as she could get her breath. "I remember you at the stall. How did you know where we lived?"

"Your father told me," said Faith. "He said you had seen my father go by, and I wanted to hear about it because I can't find him anywhere."

"Yes," said Matty. "It was yesterday that he went by. He's never been past before because I see everyone that goes by from my window. He had a breakfast-tin in his hand, and it was just about seven o'clock in the evening."

"Are you quite sure?" said little Faith.

"Yes, quite sure," said Matty, "as sure as sure can be. There isn't a many men as have only got one arm, and I know his face so well, too."

"I wonder if he'll come again?" said Faith, trembling with excitement. "If he does, Matty, do you think you could rap at the window and stop him, and tell him where I live, and how much I want to find him?"

"Aye! I'll do that," said Matty. "It's nice to be able to do anything for anyone."

"Yes," said little Faith. "It must be dreadful to lie still all day. Are you always alone, Matty?"

"Yes, till father comes in," she said. "But I tidies up the room and makes all nice before he goes. He puts all ready for me on this little table close beside me, and Mrs. Evans, who lives upstairs, comes in sometimes. She is very good; she boils my kettle on her fire."

"But you must be very lonely," said Faith.

"Oh, not so very lonely," said Matty. "I've got my books," and she pulled out two or three well-read books from under her pillow. "And then you know, Faith," she added in a lower tone, "*Jesus never goes away.*"

"Do you love Him?" asked little Faith.

"Yes," said Matty, "very much. But I didn't love Him before I was ill. I was in Miss Carter's class in the Sunday school, and, oh, how she did talk to us about coming to Jesus, and loving Jesus, and I never listened much; but when I was ill, then I thought about it all. Miss Carter often comes to see me, and she lends me such beautiful books, and she talks to me so nice when she comes."

"Will you never be any better?" asked Faith.

"Never any better till I die," said Matty. "I shall be quite well then. Miss Carter found me the verses; I'll read you them. I put a marker in the places. This is the first; it's in Isaiah: 'And the inhabitant' (that means the people that live in heaven) 'shall not say, I am sick: the people that dwell therein shall be forgiven their iniquity.' Miss Carter says that last bit is the best part of all. And here's the other; it's in Revelation: 'There shall be no more death, neither sorrow, nor crying, neither shall there be anymore pain.' Isn't that a good thing?"

"Yes, very," said Faith. " How soon do you think you'll go there, Matty?"

"I don't know," said the child. "The doctor didn't say. I would like to go very soon. I should like to go today, only there's father. Poor father! He has got nobody but me; whatever will he do when I go away?" and Matty began to cry.

"I expect Jesus will come and take care of him," said Faith.

"Yes," said Matty, "I hope so. That's why I want father so much to love Jesus; and, do you know, I think he does love Him a little, Faith. Sometimes of a night now he reads to me out of my Testament, and he likes me to talk about it now; and oh, I do pray for him so very often."

"Then the answer is sure to come," said Faith. "Mrs. Fraser always says so. I keep on praying to find my father. Sometimes I think I never shall find him, but she tells me I must wait God's time."

It was a lovely September evening, the sun was beginning to set, and the attic windows of the high houses opposite looked as if they were on fire, as the bright golden sunlight fell upon them.

Suddenly, as they were speaking, Matty raised herself quickly. She had been looking out of the window as they were talking, and now she gazed earnestly down the street.

"Yes," she cried, "it is he! There he is, Faith, coming down the street! Run, Faith, run!"

Little Faith did not need to be told twice. In a moment she had jumped up, opened the door, and run into the street.

Had the answer really come? Was her prayer heard?

Yes, there was no doubt of it. There, coming down the street to meet her, in his working clothes, with his breakfast-tin in his hand, was her father—her father whom she had lost so long.

Would he know her, or would he pass her by as if she were a stranger? Little Faith hurried on, and in another minute she was close to her father.

8

A Work for Little Faith

$\mathcal{Y}$es, he did know her. When Faith was close up to him, her father saw her. He started with surprise for a moment, and then he took her up in his arms and kissed her.

"Why, Faith, my little Faith!" he said. "I thought I should never find you again. Where have you been?"

"Why father," said Faith, as well as she could for her tears, "where have you been? I thought I should never find you again. I've been looking for you all over."

Faith finds her father.

"Come away home, Faith, and I'll tell you all about it," said her father. "I needn't be at work for another half-hour yet."

So Faith ran in with a bright face to say good-bye to Matty, and then took her father's hand, and walked with him back to his house.

The children did not know Faith at all, and they had grown very much since she had seen them last. The house was very forlorn, and the children very dirty.

"There's nobody to look to them, you see," said her father, "nobody but me, and I'm tired out by the time I get home from work. And now, little Faith, wherever in the world have you been?"

So Faith told her story, how she had heard what Mrs. Gubbins had said about taking the bread out of the children's mouths, and how she had gone to look for a little place where she could be a servant, and earn money for herself. She told him of her weary search that long, tiring day, and then how in the evening she had come to peep at him from the church porch, and how she had longed to spend her penny at the stall, that he might have one more penny to take home to Mrs. Gubbins.

Her father fairly broke down when Faith came to this part of her story.

"Bless you, bless you, child!" he said. "To think of you peeping out of the window at me! Why, if I'd only known you were there, wouldn't I have run and brought you out! I was looking for you all the time."

Then Faith went on to tell him how she had heard the singing and had gone into the church and how Mrs. Fraser had taken her home. And then she gave him an account of her happy home, and how she was being trained to be a useful servant.

"But oh, father," said little Faith, "I've been praying every day to find you, and Mrs. Fraser said the answer would come. Where have you been all this long time?"

"Well, Faith," he said, "my story's soon told. I was real cut up when I heard Mrs. Gubbins say that about you, and I made up my mind I would turn her out as soon as I woke in the morning. And then morning came, and I got up, and you were gone. I never was so angry in all my life, bairn. I told Mrs. Gubbins it was all her fault and she might go. But she said no, she wasn't going; she should stay as long as she liked.

"Well, child, I didn't know what to do. I walked up and down all day, looking for you, but I couldn't find you. Then at night I had to go to my stall, and I looked up and down the street, but I couldn't see nothing of you. And then I went home, and Mrs. Gubbins was worse drunk than ever, and she'd been beating the children. All looked so wretched without you, Faith, and I didn't know what to do. Well, on Sunday it was the same, and Monday too. Mrs. Gubbins would not turn out, and I couldn't get rid of her, and I was terrified at leaving her with the children when I was out. So on the Tuesday I only went half a day to the stall, and then, after looking about for a while, I found a man at a little toy shop in a back street who wanted some toys, and I sold him mine cheap. Then I sold my handcart to a man who I knew was looking out for one.

"Well, I put the money in my pocket and went home, and Mrs. Gubbins was out. *Now*, I thought, is the time. Mrs. Gubbins won't go away from us, so we'll go away from her. So I gathered up the children's bits of clothes as quick as I could, and anything I could get hold of, and we were off before Mrs. Gubbins came back. I had seen in the newspaper that they wanted a man to carry parcels at a shop in Wingtown, that's six miles from here. Well, we went there, and I got taken on; but it was hard work and small pay. I stopped there till last week, though. Then I heard they were advertising for night-watchmen at the docks here, to go on board the steamers that are in port, and keep watch of a night. So I wrote and applied, and my master gave me a character, and they told me I might come. They pay me good wages, and I might be very comfortable, but there's nobody to do anything. I've got a few bits of furniture in, but all's in a muddle yet. I must get it righted up next week. I don't think Mrs. Gubbins will find us out here; it's a good long way from Belfry Row."

"Oh, no," said Faith, "she'll never find you out. Don't you know Mrs. Gubbins is dead, father?"

John Robinson was very shocked to hear this. Faith gave him an account of her visit to the attic and of the dreadful sight she had seen there.

Then it was time for her father to go to his work and for Faith to go back to her mistress. Oh, with what a happy heart the child went home. Ellen guessed the good news by Faith's bright face, even before she had had time to speak a word. And no one was more pleased than Mrs. Fraser.

"Now, little Faith," she said, "has not God been good to you? Let us thank Him together."

So the old lady and Faith knelt down, and with very grateful hearts gave thanks to the Lord for His gracious answer to their prayers.

The next morning Mrs. Fraser went to see the minister and had a long talk with him about what little Faith was to do. At first Mr. Barker was very anxious that she should remain with Mrs. Fraser, where she had such a happy home and so many advantages. But when Mrs. Fraser reminded him how good John Robinson had been to the child, how he had taken her into his home and family when she was a little friendless orphan, and how he had always treated her and loved her as his own child, he agreed with the old lady that now, when her father really needed her help, and when she was old enough to be of some use to him, it was only right that Faith should do what she could to pay back, in some measure, all that her father had done for her.

When Mrs. Fraser came home, she talked it over with Faith and gave the little girl leave to go home at the end of the week, and, if her father wished it, to stay with him and take care of the house and children.

So early on Saturday morning little Faith set off for her new home, with an earnest prayer in her heart that she might indeed be a blessing there. It was about eight o'clock when she arrived there. Mrs. Fraser had let her go early because it was Saturday, and she thought she would be able to make the house more comfortable for her father before Sunday.

When Faith arrived, she was received with shouts of joy by the children. They were playing in the middle of the floor, drawing pictures with cinders, and making it, if possible, blacker than ever.

The fireplace was choked with ashes and looked as if it had not been swept for days. The walls were covered with cobwebs and dust, for the house had been shut up for some time before they came to it and had never been cleaned since they arrived. The table was covered with dirty cups and plates, and the floor was strewn with clothes, and pans, and brushes, and broken toys. It looked very forlorn and hopeless.

"Where's father?" said Faith to the children.

"He's asleep in bed. He gets home at seven, and then he goes to bed, and wakes up about two o'clock, and then he comes down and gets us some dinner."

"Let's make the room tidy and nice," said Faith, "before father wakes. Who'll help me?"

The children thought it great fun to help Faith in her cleaning. She put on a large apron, and soon they were very busy.

They turned everything out of the kitchen into the little yard at the back of the house, and then Faith took a long brush and swept the ceiling and the walls. Then she sent the children for some blacklead and pipe clay, and blackleaded the stove and cleaned the hearth.

The children got quite excited as the work went on and really made themselves very useful. Then the floor was washed, the window cleaned, the table scoured, and the chairs dusted and polished.

"It does look beautiful!" said Fanny, when their work was done and Faith had lighted the fire and put on the kettle.

"Now about dinner," said Faith, as she looked with satisfaction at her work. "What time is it?"

Tommy ran to the corner of the street to look at the church clock and came back to say it was only eleven. Faith had some money of her own in her pocket, so she went out and made her little purchases. She bought some pieces of meat and some vegetables to make into good soup, such as she had so often watched Ellen making, and some apples for dumplings for the children.

"Now, then," she said to them, when all was in train for dinner, "we must smarten *you* up a bit."

This was a more difficult business than even the house, but Faith took a large basin into the yard and washed them well, and combed and cut and brushed their hair, and made them look very different from what they had done when she came in.

"We must have a wash on Monday," said Faith, "and get all your clothes clean and tidy."

There was no time to do more now; she could hear her father moving upstairs, for it was nearly two o'clock. Faith quite shook with excitement when she heard him coming downstairs.

John Robinson came into the room, and then stood still, mute with astonishment.

"Well, I never!" he said, at length. "I wouldn't have known the place! Bless me, Faith, darling, have *you* done it? Well, it's just like when Mary was alive!"

"I hope it will look much nicer soon, father," said Faith. "I must get the children's clothes done next week."

"You don't mean to say you're going to stop, Faith!" said her father, as he sat down to eat his nicely prepared dinner.

"Yes, father, if you'll have me," said little Faith.

"Have you, my lass," he said, "*have* you? Why, you're my little comforter! Haven't I been longing to have you this great while? But I don't like to take you from such a good home."

"Father," said little Faith, as she got up and kissed him, "do you think I could ever forget all you've done for me? And I want so much to show you how I love you for it."

That was the beginning of many happy days for John Robinson and his children. Faith was in every way his little comforter. She kept his house in beautiful order and the children clean and tidy.

Above all, she tried to lead him in the way to heaven.

Mrs. Fraser and Ellen often came to see her and helped her in every way. And Faith felt that if she went to them, she could always find sympathy in her troubles and advice in her difficulties. She was also able to be a great comfort to little Matty, who lived very near them, and to help to nurse her until she went to the city where there is no more pain.

Little Faith never forgot her text. Mr. Barker printed it for her in large and clear letters, and Mrs. Fraser gave her a frame in which to hang it.

It was put up on the wall in the kitchen where everyone could see it. And whenever Faith was downcast, or troubled, or anxious, and whenever her prayers did not seem to be answered, she glanced up from her work at the text on the wall, and she heard her Lord once more asking her the question, "O thou of little faith, wherefore didst thou doubt?"

The End